The Three Little Elephants

Adapted by Michelle Jovin, M.A.

Illustrated by Sharon Vargo

Inree Elephunts

three home ideas

hay and stick

a rock home

6 "Oh no! a hungry lion

8 "oh no"

arocknome

Publishing Credits

Rachelle Cracchiolo, M.S.Ed., *Publisher*
Conni Medina, M.A.Ed., *Editor in Chief*
Nika Fabienke, Ed.D., *Content Director*
Véronique Bos, *Creative Director*
Shaun Bernadou, *Art Director*
Michelle Jovin, M.A., *Associate Editor*
Jess Johnson, *Graphic Designer*

Image Credits: Illustrations by Sharon Vargo.

Library of Congress Control Number: 2019937938

TCM | Teacher
Created
Materials

5301 Oceanus Drive
Huntington Beach, CA 92649-1030
www.tcmpub.com
ISBN 978-1-6449-1286-7
© 2020 Teacher Created Materials, Inc.
Printed in China
Nordica.052019.CA21900843